MW00916225

RIVER OF LIGHTS

The Magic Portal Series

MELANIE DOBSON

Ember Roth Books

THE MAGIC PORTAL

Elizabeth Quinsland

Thank you for inspiring me
to take this journey into the Land of Light.

Thief!

"IT'S MAGICAL," Katie whispered as she gazed down from the deck of the Eiffel Tower. The evening lights on both sides of river Seine twinkled like fireflies.

Norah, the girl standing next to her, snickered. "You think everything is magical."

Katie turned slowly toward Norah so she wouldn't bump her ankle cast against the wall. Norah's long black hair hung straight over the shoulders of her white blouse, her glossy lips pressed into a smirk. The rest of the girls from their class were huddled around a banned cell phone instead of looking at the lights.

"I was just thinking—" Katie started.

Norah crossed her arms. "What were you thinking?"

"That it would be fun to swim under all the lights."

Norah rolled her eyes. "That river is filthy!"

"But if it was clean, it would be wonderful."

"You are ridiculous," Norah said before moving away to join their classmates.

Katie wrapped her fingers around the pink sapphire on her necklace, her stomach turning. What was wrong with enjoying the lights?

The other boarding school girls didn't like her much, but it was much better to think Paris was magical than to think—well, to think everything was miserable here.

She missed her home in Oregon. Missed her horse and her grandparents and the friends who were kind to her.

The girls rushed to the other side of the deck, and Katie slowly followed. She couldn't move fast with the cast over her ankle. The doctor in Oregon said it would take months to recover from the fall off her horse. He didn't know when the pain would go away.

It was just one more thing that made her different from the girls at school.

Her gaze drifted back over the edge of the platform. The beauty of this city and all its color and life were a welcome break from the teasing of Norah and her other classmates.

In the background, Katie heard a tour guide speaking in English.

"Six million people gathered here in 1900 for the World's Fair. Many of them would ride up this tower to look at the spectacle of exhibits across Paris. The most popular exhibit was right there."

The guide pointed down at a field between the tower and river, and Katie's head began to spin. She clutched a banister down the middle of the deck as she stepped away from the edge. Sometimes heights made her dizzy, and she didn't want to feel sick now, not with her classmates already thinking she was strange.

"The Palace of Electricity," the guide announced as if it was royal. "Inside the building was a fairy-land of lights and on top was a giant statue called the Light Fairy."

Katie's mind wandered as she looked away from the city lights, wondering what this fairyland must have looked like more than a hundred years ago. Her hand swept up to the tear-dropped sapphire again, imagining how it might glow in a palace of lights. On this cool evening, the stone felt warm on her skin.

"What happened to the Palace of Electricity?" a woman asked. She, like everyone else in the tour group, wore a black beret with a bright green ribbon attached to it.

Katie leaned in for the answer, but instead she heard the voice of her headmistress.

"Come along," Miss Marguerite commanded, oblivious to the tour group. "We must hurry or we'll be late to the Louvre." The famous art museum was opening tonight for an evening tour.

Norah hid the cell phone behind her back as Miss Marguerite waved the girls toward the elevator. Katie clutched the railing that led to the elevators, trying to ignore the pain that shot up from her injured ankle.

Her classmates crammed into the elevator with the tour guide and group of tourists with their bulky cameras and matching berets. At first, Katie was afraid they'd leave without her, but Norah turned back. Katie waved her hand like Miss Marguerite so Norah would keep the elevator door open.

Instead Norah looked straight at her and pushed a button.

"Wait!" Katie called out as the doors closed. She stared at the elevator door then looked across the empty platform. What was she supposed to do now? Her leg ached and she felt...

In that moment, she felt terribly alone.

Shivering, Katie reached again for the sapphire on her necklace as if it could summon her father.

When they moved to France, her dad had given her a cell phone so she could call him in an emergency, but he was currently on an airplane headed back from a meeting in England. She couldn't call him, and she couldn't call her teacher. Miss Marguerite didn't own a mobile phone nor did she condone the use of them among her charges.

Surely Miss Marguerite would realize Katie was missing before their class left on the bus. Her teacher would be irritated, thinking Katie had been distracted instead of staying with her group. It was pointless to tell her about Norah. The girl had perfected the role of teacher's pet, but even if she hadn't, Norah's mom worked for the Prime Minister. Miss Marguerite would never reprimand her.

In the month since they'd moved to France, Katie had wanted to tell her dad how mean the other girls were, but she only saw him on the weekends. Last time she'd tried to talk to him about school, his cell phone had rang, interrupting their breakfast talk. He'd forgotten about their discussion as he rushed into his office.

The truth was—they were both distracted.

Katie's mother had left them twelve years ago, in the months after Katie was born, and never returned. Her dad rarely spoke about his wife Liana, and Katie stopped asking questions a long time ago. But this city rekindled all of the questions about her mother. She only had one picture of her parents together, both of them smiling outside a café in Paris after her dad asked Liana to marry him. When they were both happy.

Sometimes she seemed to feel her mother's presence in this city, especially in the lights along the river.

Katie blinked back her tears.

If only her best friend was here. She and Paige would link arms and say *chalk-out-loud* instead of *chocolat* and then laugh when they butchered the French word. They'd ignore every mean girl and watch the fairy lights of Paris together.

The elevator chimed, and Katie hobbled toward it.

Had Miss Marguerite or one of the girls returned for her?

The door opened, but the elevator was empty. Stepping inside, Katie pressed the button for the first floor. The glass elevator crept slowly downwards, stopping twice to let in more people before they reached the bottom.

As Katie limped out onto the grass, she glanced around at a crowd of people from all over the world. Some were taking pictures, others holding hands as they gazed at the river like they thought the lights were magical as well.

Miss Marguerite had warned them about a ring

of thieves who stole cameras and jewelry from tourists, but Katie didn't have anything to steal except her necklace. She tucked it under the collar of her sweatshirt.

A man with crutches hobbled along the river walk. He wore a dark sweater and on his head was a black beret. One of the English tourists, she thought, except he had no ribbon attached to his cap.

As she scanned the row of buses for her class-mates and then the tourist boats on a dock below, she wondered how the man had injured his leg. She'd never know, of course, but perhaps he'd fallen from a horse too.

Nearby a man in a brown leather jacket knelt beside a woman dressed in an elegant red evening gown, Katie's gaze froze on the couple.

Was he going to propose?

Her mind drifted again to the picture of her parents here in Paris. Had her dad gotten down on one knee when he asked Liana to marry him? If she'd wanted to get married, why had she left their family after Katie was born?

"Chloe—" The man pulled out a small box and opened it.

The woman clapped her hands together when she saw the ring inside.

"Will you marry me?" the man asked.

Chloe smiled, and Katie couldn't help but smile

along with her. Hopefully, their love would last forever.

"Kathryn!" Miss Marguerite called behind her.

Before she turned back, Katie watched with dismay as the man in the beret stumbled on the sidewalk. He and his crutches fell on top of the man trying to propose.

"There you are," Miss Marguerite scolded her. "We have no time to waste."

"But there's been an accident." Katie pointed at the men sprawled on the sidewalk. How unfortunate for the one with the injured leg. And for the man trying to ask his girlfriend to marry him.

"Kathryn Andrews," Miss Marguerite said without even glancing at the men. "We've no time for make-believe either."

"I'm not making it up," Katie insisted, wishing her teacher would stop treating her like she was two. All Miss Marguerite had to do was look down at the river.

Instead, Miss Marguerite tugged on Katie's arm, and she reluctantly followed her teacher toward the bus.

A man shouted, "My ring!"

Katie turned back and saw the gentleman in the leather jacket still on his knees, but this time he was searching the ground. Then the pretty woman—Chloe—dropped to her knees beside him.

Katie's heart raced as she looked for the man with the crutches. Perhaps he knew where the ring went.

Miss Marguerite directed all the girls toward the bus, but Katie didn't move. When her teacher stepped onto the bus, Katie limped back toward the couple.

"It's his grandmother's engagement ring," Chloe said, tears in her eyes.

Katie nodded. She would help them find it. Then she would walk to the Louvre.

In the streetlights, she searched the crowds until she saw the man with the black beret. He was down by the tourist boats except this time he was walking without crutches.

Katie's heart began to race again.

Had he taken the ring?

She glanced back at the bus one more time. Her dad would tell her to stay with the group, to be safe, but he wouldn't want a thief to go free either.

Somehow she would figure out a way to join her classmates at the art museum. Right now, she needed to find out if the man with the beret had stolen Chloe's ring.

Secret Window

THE MAN with the beret jumped into the river. At least, that's what it looked like to Katie as she hobbled down to the riverside.

The evening lights must be blurring her vision. Even though she might dream about swimming in the river, Norah was right—the water smelled terrible. She'd never jump into it.

When she reached the dock, Katie saw two long tour boats tied up along the wall, and another boat was traveling under the bridge to her right. On the busy road above was a crowd of pedestrians and the clamor of honking horns, but she was alone on the platform.

The lights from the Eiffel Tower poured over her as she crept to the edge. Maybe the man had jumped into one of the waiting boats instead of the river. If he stole the ring, he might wait here for hours until Chloe and her boyfriend had given up their search.

But she knew he was down here someplace. Once she found him, she would call for help. Or perhaps she should call now.

Her dad would tell her to call.

Katie reached for her back pocket and took out her cell phone. Dad had keyed in the emergency number at the top of her contact list.

She squeezed her eyes before dialing. What was the French word for *thief*? Her instructor hadn't taught her it yet.

Somehow she would have to make the operator understand.

When she reopened her eyes, a light flashed below her feet. At first she thought the tower lights were reflecting in the water, but then the lights began to cluster together into bubbles on the surface.

Mesmerized, she lowered her phone.

The lights weren't just the golden color from the streetlamps or the Eiffel Tower. They flickered with a deep midnight blue and a sparkly green and a pumpkin orange color that reminded her of Miss Marguerite's lipstick.

A loud splash startled her, and when she turned back, the bubbles and lights in the river seemed to mold into a face. For the briefest moment, she thought she saw the man with the black beret looking back at her from under the surface.

Shivering, she squeezed her eyes closed again and shook her head. Of course there was no man under the water. Was it his reflection on the surface? Whirling on her good foot, she looked to see if he was behind her, but no one was there.

Her shoulders slumped as she zipped her phone back into her pocket. Miss Marguerite was right about the make believe. The engagement ring must have been lost in the grass, not stolen by a thief.

Katie glanced back at the river. The lights grew even brighter, exploding like fireworks below her feet. Was she imagining all the colors like she'd imagined the man in the beret?

Her head spun, and she pressed her eyes closed as the lights blurred together in her mind. Blue. Green. Orange. She started to open her eyes again when…

A shock of cold pierced her skin.

She was no longer standing on the dock. She was in the river! Her entire body soaking wet.

Somehow she'd fallen into the Seine.

She screamed as she sank, but the water just bubbled around her. Her arms flailing, she tried to kick her feet, but the cast on her ankle dragged her farther down, her leg throbbing.

The colors flickered even brighter as she fought

the current, but she kept sinking until her arm struck something hard. In the river beside her was a stone wall. And a window.

Water flowed through an iron grate across the window, and on the other side, she could see trees. Perhaps she could get to the surface through here.

Her good foot pressed against the stone wall, Katie yanked open the window grate and swam through a short tunnel until she reached the other side. Her lungs burning, she broke through the surface seconds later and gasped a deep breath as she treaded water.

The river bank was only a few feet away, and she paddled toward it, wading out of the water. Then she collapsed onto a flat rock, her hands splayed out to her sides as she breathed in the warm air. The gentle breeze. The quiet.

Her eyes bolted open again. It shouldn't be quiet.

She looked up, expecting to see the Eiffel Tower, but nothing was familiar around her.

Where was she? And where was the man with the black beret?

Inching herself up, she looked at a forest to her left. There were no golden city lights on this part of the river. No boats or tourists or buses. In fact, she was quite alone along the grassy bank. A ceiling of leaves hid most of the river as the stream wove back through the trees.

The colorful display of lights were gone, but a white light blinked across a grassy field above the river bank, inside a building. At first, she thought it was a barn, but it seemed to be some sort of mill. A wooden waterwheel circled slowly on the side of the building, the water splashing into the river like waves lapping against a shore.

Katie reached for her necklace, relieved to find it still there. Then she pulled out her cell phone. In spite of the water, her phone still worked, but she didn't have service. Her dad wouldn't be happy. She was supposed to be able to use this phone anyplace in Paris. She'd have to make her way to the art museum—or at least back to the Eiffel Tower—on her own.

Standing up, she began to walk through the tall river grass, toward the mill. Perhaps she could use a telephone inside to call her dad.

The grass tickled her feet, and several steps later, she realized that not only was her shoe gone, her ankle cast had disappeared too.

Did she lose those in the river? It was odd—her ankle didn't hurt at all now and even her limp was gone, as if she'd lost it with her cast in the Seine.

It had been months since she'd been able to walk without pain, ever since a snake startled her horse back in Oregon. Thankfully, her horse hadn't been injured when he threw Katie off, but the doctor said she couldn't ride again until her ankle healed. Katie had been relieved. As much as she loved to ride, she'd been afraid to get back on a horse.

She scrunched up her bare toes in the grass, glad to be rid of her cast, and kept walking. When she reached the weathered walls of the mill, the water-wheel creaked another round beside her, then it stopped running. There were no windows on the building, but light seeped out around the doorframe and between cracks in the wood.

Inside was a buzzing noise, and then she heard the urgent voice of a girl. "We need more!"

"It's too dangerous to go back up now," a man replied.

Katie leaned closer—was that the man who took the ring?

"You and the others must go again," the girl said. "First thing in the morning."

The white light dimmed, and when the door crept open, Katie hid under the shadow of the wheel.

The girl stepped outside and walked slowly toward the river. Katie waited for the man to follow her, but he stayed inside the mill.

What did this girl need more of?

Katie couldn't see what the girl was wearing, but she watched her sit on the same rock where Katie had rested. And then the girl began to cry.

Katie understood the tears—it sounded as if she might be lonely as well.

While Katie wanted to comfort the girl, she didn't move. Until she found out what happened, she'd stay hidden in the shadows.

Firefly Princess

KATIE DIDN'T MOVE from her hiding place until after the girl stepped into a small boat and rowed away. The white light had faded into a dull glow, and Katie crept forward to look into this glassy thread of the river—so different from the busy Seine on the other side of the window grate.

It hadn't been very deep in this section of the river. Now that her ankle wasn't hurting, perhaps she could swim down and find the window again. Then she'd swim back up to the boat platform and make her way to the bus or the Louvre.

Miss Marguerite must be looking everywhere for her.

Dipping her toes into the warm water, she waded into the river, but without the colorful lights, she couldn't see anything under the surface. She'd never be able to find the window in the dark.

Disappointed, she returned to the shore. She would have to wait for the morning light to find the passage back. Miss Marguerite would be in a panic, but there was nothing else she could do—it wasn't like she'd tried to fall into the water.

All she had to do was stay calm. Pretend like she was back home in Oregon, taking an evening walk with her dad and her grandmother on a summer night.

Clutching her arms across her chest, she searched the night sky. She couldn't see either the moon or stars, but something was blinking in the forest to her left. A pale green light, like one of the colors she'd seen in the river.

Then something blinked blue.

Was there a road on the other side of these trees?

She walked along the river until she reached the edge of the forest, but instead of the sound of cars, she heard someone whispering.

"Who is she?" a woman asked.

"She looks like the princess," another woman replied.

"The princess wouldn't come here. It's much too dangerous."

"Perhaps she is lost?"

"Perhaps the queen has banished her from the palace."

"She doesn't look well—"

Katie put her hands on her hips. "I can hear you."

The voices silenced.

The Queen of England had visited Paris last month, and Miss Marguerite had practically lost her mind in the days before the queen arrived, interrogating the girls for hours on their etiquette as if Her Majesty might pay a royal visit to their school. But her teacher hadn't mentioned another royal visit. Perhaps the princess was visiting in secret.

The green light flickered again, and she wondered if the people in the forest were carrying colored lanterns. "Are you Princess Lilly?" someone asked.

"No—my name is Katie."

"Her name is Katie," several people whispered.

A woman cleared her throat. "Where do you come from, Katie?"

"Oregon."

More whispering. "We've never heard of Oregon."

She sighed. "Most people around here have never heard of it."

"How many years are you?" the woman asked.

"I'm twelve."

An orange light joined the blue and green ones, and this time a man spoke, his voice much gruffer than the women. "Who have you been talking to, Katie from Oregon?"

"I—" Katie started, confused. She thought about the girls in her class. Miss Marguerite. All the people they'd met on their outings. How was she supposed to begin naming all the people she'd met in France? "I talk to a lot of people."

The man drew closer. "What sort of people?"

More lights joined them. Katie squinted, trying to see who carried the lanterns, but she couldn't see anything beyond the light, not even their faces.

"Lamont," another voice said, this one a woman who sounded much kinder. "We will discuss this later."

The other voices murmured their agreement.

"Come along, child," the kind woman said.

Katie hesitated. "Can you help me get to the Louvre?"

"The lube?"

"No, the art museum," she said. "In Paris."

A wind blew through the leaves, rustling them. It sent a cold chill over her skin.

"We must hurry, child."

As the lights moved away, Katie expected to hear footsteps, but all she heard were the leaves. The rustling sound grew louder as if someone was shaking a fistful of branches.

She shivered in the wind, wondering again where the man in the black beret had gone. She wasn't supposed to leave with strangers, but it also wasn't safe to spend the night alone in this forest.

Quietly she followed the light of the kind woman into the trees until they reached the biggest tree Katie had ever seen. She scanned the branches behind it, searching for some sort of house. The tree creaked, and she watched in amazement as the bark in front of her peeled back. On the other side was a door.

Leaning forward, Katie saw the shadows of a small fire dancing inside its hollow. Then she looked behind her to see the three people who accompanied her. Except there were no people. Only black insects, each the size of a football. Each one blinking a different color.

She swallowed her scream. "You're—you're flies."

The one with the pale green light shook her head. "We're fireflies."

"Still," Katie muttered. "Fireflies can't talk."

"Perhaps not in your Oregon or Paris, but we can certainly talk here."

"You most of all," the one with a man's voice said, his orange light flickering.

The green firefly hushed him. "Don't be mean, Lamont."

"But I'm in Paris!" Katie insisted.

Lamont's wings buzzed as he lifted off the ground. "She's confused."

"No, I'm not." Katie crossed her arms over her chest, but even when she said the words, she wondered if the firefly was right. She was more than confused. She was in a strange new world, talking to a firefly.

Maybe she'd fallen on the dock and hit her head. Soon she'd awaken to see Miss Marguerite or maybe even her father hovering over her.

Did her dad know she was gone?

"I'm Isabel," the firefly with the green light said. "You look like Princess Lilly."

"She's too thin to be the princess," one of them muttered.

"I think she's too fat."

"I'm not too anything," Katie said.

The leaves rustled again and Isabel stretched out her arms, waving Katie into the opening of the oak tree. "We must get in before he comes."

"Before who comes?" Katie asked as she stepped inside.

Fireflies buzzed past her into the hollow, and Isabel closed the door behind them. Her green light blinking, Isabel motioned Katie down a spiral staircase made of roots. "We will wait here until morning."

Katie ducked under the beam and started to descend the staircase toward the firelight. Both sides were papered with worn stripes that trailed down the steps, like the faded colors of a rainbow.

She turned back to Isabel. "Where am I?"

"This is our home."

"I mean—" she began with a shake of her head. "You said you've never heard of Paris."

"Oh, we've heard of Paris," Isabel said, the green light pulsing along with her words. "Just not your Oregon."

"So if we're not in Paris—where are we?"

"Our world is called Rodenia."

Katie's head spun. Perhaps she had fallen asleep on the bus ride to the Louvre. She must be in some sort of a dream.

"We need to rest," Isabel said. "The morning will be busy for all of us."

"What happens in the morning?" she asked.

"We go hunting with the others."

Katie rubbed her arms. "What do you hunt for?"

Isabel lowered her voice. "We hunt for light."

Spies

A LOUD BUZZ WOKE KATIE, and she threw off her blanket, swinging her legs onto the floor in the dark bedroom. She was scheduled to help in the school's kitchen this morning, and it sounded like the cook had started making breakfast without her.

If Miss Marguerite found out she was late, Katie would have to spend an entire week working in the kitchen.

She'd had the weirdest dream last night of a strange world underneath the river. A place with talking fireflies and a maze of rooms below a giant oak tree. A world where her ankle didn't ache and the girls from school couldn't tease her.

In her dream, she'd sipped a hot drink that tasted of strawberries and cream as she stood by a fire, wearing a soft robe as she waited for her clothes to dry. Lamont, who seemed to be the oldest firefly, brought her a pair of slip-on shoes to replace her cast and the shoe that she'd lost in the river.

Even now, as she reached for her clothes, her ankle didn't hurt. She'd ask Miss Marguerite to call her doctor after breakfast to see if she could walk on it now.

A light flickered on the wall outside her room and she smiled as she remembered the colorful lights in her dream. Part of her wished she could curl back on her bed and return to the world of fireflies, just for a few minutes before she faced the mean girls at her school.

But the cook would start banging the pans even louder if she didn't hurry. There'd be no more sleeping this morning.

She dressed quickly and slipped out the door, expecting to see the long hallway in the dormitory.

Instead there was a living room on the other side.

Katie grasped for the wall to balance herself, clenching one of the tree roots that threaded around the room. In front of her was a couch covered in a glittery yellow and blue. Behind the couch was a black grate that contained the glow of the fire. Dozens of tiny flowers were carved into the stone mantle above it.

In front of the fireplace, a group of fireflies

huddled together, whispering their secrets like they'd done in the forest last night.

Perhaps this wasn't a dream after all. Perhaps she had really gotten herself trapped in another world where fireflies could talk.

How was she going to get back to Paris?

This morning she would walk back to the river and find the river wall and its window. By now, Miss Marguerite would have called her dad, and he would be terrified. The French police would be searching all along the river for her.

She had to leave right away.

Katie cleared her throat. "Excuse me."

The whispering stopped as the beaded eyes of six fireflies turned toward her.

In that moment, she realized their lights were no longer blinking brightly. Instead Isabel had a faint green glow that looked more like an iridescent sash. Lamont's orange light had turned into a brownish ring around his waist.

"I—" Katie glanced between Lamont and Isabel. "I need to go back to the river."

The whispering started again, and she had to step closer to hear what they were saying.

"It's not safe outside," the firefly with a purple light said. "Not safe at all."

"But we must take her back."

"We'll go later, Isabel." Lamont stirred the fire. "Much later."

Katie interrupted them. "But I can't go any later. My dad will be looking for me."

Lamont shook his head. "It can't be helped. We have to leave here within the hour."

Katie remembered Isabel's words from last night. "Can I help you hunt for light?"

Then they could take her to the river.

"Perhaps—" one of the fireflies began, but Lamont stopped him.

"It's too dangerous for you to catch light."

She reached for her necklace and began to rub the sapphire, the pink jewel glowing red in the fire-light. There had to be a way to get out of here.

Isabel crept closer. "What is that?"

Surprised, Katie quickly tucked the sapphire back under her shirt. "My mother gave it to me when I was a baby."

"Did she say her mother?" one of the fireflies whispered.

"Her mother."

They huddled together again. "How is that possible?"

"Perhaps she—" another started, but then stopped before she finished her sentence. "Do you think it could be?"

"Of course not."

"But it's possible—"

"We can take her jewel," the purple firefly said.

Katie cupped her hand over her collar. "You most certainly cannot."

The firefly drew closer, but Lamont flew in front of Katie, his wings outstretched to protect her. "We aren't taking anything."

The chattering ended, and Katie realized they were all staring at her now, their black eyes wide.

Lamont landed on the edge of a chair. "Where is this mother of yours?"

Katie shook her head. "I don't know."

"Did she leave your world?"

"She left *me*. When I was a baby," Katie said with a shrug, trying to act like it didn't matter that Liana Andrews had disappeared.

The words sparked another round of discussion, and Katie knew she must get out of the tree. She couldn't listen to these strangers—fireflies, no less—discussing the whereabouts of her mother. Katie couldn't even remember what her mother looked like beyond the blurry picture in Paris or the sound of her voice or if she'd ever loved her daughter.

She turned back toward the staircase. "I have to go home."

Isabel flew up beside her. "Before you leave, Lamont and I will take you to visit Princess Lilly."

"I thought you were going to hunt."

Isabel shook her head. "The others will hunt for us today."

Bewildered, Katie followed Isabel and Lamont up the knobby staircase and back outside. Even though it was morning, the forest was almost as dark as it had been last night.

How could she get back to Paris without the light to guide her?

Katie squinted up at the dark sky. "When does the sun come out?"

"We have no sun in the Land of Light," Isabel said.

She didn't know it was possible to live without the sun. "I thought this world was called Rodenia."

"Ours is only one of the lands in Rodenia."

"Where do you get light?" Katie asked.

Lamont's tiny hand covered his mouth. "We mustn't speak of it," he mumbled.

"Why not?"

"Sometimes Gaul sends his spies to patrol the woods."

A hundred more questions popped into Katie's mind—about the princess and this Gaul and what exactly would happen if one of these spies found them—but she stayed silent.

This land of fireflies may not have a sun or even a moon, but some sort of light had cast dull shadows over the river last night and across the forest floor.

Once they reached the edge of the trees, her two escorts stopped and Katie listened alongside them. In the distance she could see the mill, the wheel slowly rotating as it poured water into the river.

She'd been waiting for daylight to find the tunnel back into Paris, but it seemed as if the light would never come. She had no choice. The window into the river Seine couldn't be far below the surface. She would have to search in the darkness until she found it.

A light flickered in the mill, and Isabel squealed.

"Quiet," Lamont commanded before motioning them forward. "We must hurry."

Lamont looked both ways before flying into a meadow, but Katie didn't follow him or Isabel this time.

Lamont turned back toward her. "We can't stay here, Miss Katie."

"I know." Her gaze remained on the river. "But I can't go with you either."

"You must," Isabel insisted, panic lacing her voice. "We need your help."

"I wish I could help, but I'm afraid there's nothing I can do." She motioned toward the water. "I need to find my way back to Paris."

"You won't be able to return the way you came." Isabel drew close to her again. "Besides, I think you might find that your home is right here."

"I belong in France," she said even though Paris didn't feel like home.

"Please come with us," Lamont said, but instead of commanding this time, he was begging.

"Princess Lilly will be able to explain everything," Isabel assured her. "Then she can help you return to Paris."

Katie glanced at the water again before looking back at the light in the mill.

Lamont nodded toward the light. "The princess is waiting for us."

Curious, she followed the fireflies toward the mill. She would find out how she could help them. Then she would ask this Princess Lilly for help getting home.

Hunting for Light

A DINOSAUR of a machine stretched across the inside of the mill, its neck climbing up to the ceiling. The dark metal groaned and shuddered as it worked, the walls of the mill trembling around Katie and all the fireflies. She watched mesmerized as the top of the machine glowed white.

Seconds later, the machine began to slow and the loud thumping sound quieted. A girl about Katie's age moved out from behind the machine, wearing a pretty teal and white gown. The same girl Katie had seen crying by the river.

The fireflies separated, their backs against both walls, but Katie stepped closer to the girl. When she saw the girl's face, they both gasped. It was as if they were looking in a mirror.

The girl's hair was more of a chestnut color than

a golden brown, but the long waves flowed over her shoulders like Katie's hair and her blue eyes were the same color as Katie's.

No wonder why the fireflies were confused. With the exception of their clothing and hair color, she and the girl before her were almost identical, as if part of her—or her reflection—lived in this world of Rodenia.

"Are you the princess?" Katie asked.

The girl nodded.

Princess Lilly studied Katie's face and then her sweatshirt and jeans before asking. "Who are you?"

"Katie Andrews," she replied. "I'm from Oregon, but I live with my dad in Paris now."

"The City of Lights," the princess whispered. "I've heard it is a beautiful place."

At first, Katie thought the princess might be teasing her like Norah had done, but she seemed sincere. "It's especially beautiful at night."

"I've always wanted to see it."

"I can take you," Katie offered.

The princess shook her head. "I can't leave Rodenia." The sadness in her eyes turned into a smile. "But it's okay. I love this land."

Katie wanted to ask Lilly what she could possibly like about this dark place, but she didn't want to offend her or the fireflies around them.

The white glow on the top of the machine began to fade, and a long shadow crept across the room.

"We need more light." Isabel moaned.

The princess turned toward her and the other fireflies. "Someone will return soon."

"We were hoping Katie could help."

The princess eyed her again. "How can you help?"

She shrugged. "I have no idea."

"Show her your necklace," Isabel prompted.

Katie tugged the gemstone out from under her collar, and when the princess saw the sapphire, her eyes grew wide. "Where did you get that?" she asked.

"It was a gift from my mother when I was a baby."

The princess slowly reached out and touched the jewel. "It is lovely."

The door to the mill opened again, and everyone stepped back into the shadows until they could see the visitor. It was another firefly, but this one had something draped over his neck.

"Very good, Bernard," the princess said.

Bernard bowed his head and pumped his wings as Lilly lifted a silver bracelet from his neck. The chain coiled into the palm of Lilly's hand, and Katie leaned over to study the jewels in the pendant. One looked like a diamond and the other was a brilliant blue color.

Katie glanced back up at Bernard. "Where did you get the bracelet?"

"Near the tower."

"The Eiffel Tower?" Katie asked.

Bernard shrugged with his wings.

"How did you get to the tower?"

"Through the river."

She started to ask about the window, but he wasn't paying attention to her now. Instead he and the other fireflies were following Lilly to the mouth of the machine. Katie watched in horror as the princess dropped the bracelet into it.

"Someone will be looking for that." Katie reached out to retrieve the bracelet, but it was too late. The machine began to groan, and then the thumping sound resumed. The white glow grew stronger with the noise and a rainbow of color surged over all of them.

Isabel began blinking green again. Lamont orange. The other fireflies joined them with brilliant yellow, silver, and purple wings.

Lilly clapped her hands together and smiled.

The colors were beautiful, but Katie remembered the faces of Chloe and her boyfriend by the Eiffel Tower when they lost their ring. She remembered the man with the black beret who'd taken it.

Whoever had lost this bracelet was probably searching frantically for it.

While the others celebrated, Katie stepped toward the princess.

"Did he steal that bracelet?" she shouted over the noise of the machine.

"Jewels come from the earth," Lilly explained.

"But in our world, the stones are made into jewelry that people buy."

The princess's smile dimmed. "None of us want to steal." She tugged at the silky sleeves of her gown. "But we have no choice. My friends won't survive without the light."

Katie eyed the machine again. "You use the jewels to make light?"

Lilly motioned toward the door, and they stepped outside. The princess sat down on one of the rocks, her teal gown rippling around her. Katie sat beside her and crossed her legs.

"My friends need the light to sustain them like you and I need food to survive. Without the light, their color fades away, and in a few days…" Lilly's voice trailed off. "My friends won't live long without the light."

"Can't you use fire instead of the jewels?" Katie asked.

Lilly shook her head. "We've already tried. Fire keeps them warm, but it doesn't give them life."

Katie rubbed her knuckles together, thinking about all the lights in Paris. "There must be another way."

"Not anymore." The princess's eyes grew sad again as she looked back toward the old mill. "Our whole land has been cursed by a wicked wizard named Gaul. He came from a dark northern land, and he hates the light and everyone who needs it to live. When he took our land, he cast a spell over our skies and our queen."

"Your mother?" Katie asked.

Lilly nodded. "My mother used to be kind to everyone in our land. She gave the most beautiful parties every spring for everyone who lived here. The valley was filled with flowers and we would dance and laugh and drink punch made from the sweet cherries in our orchard. Then a year ago, Gaul paid a secret visit to our palace. Somehow he convinced my mother into hiding the light from all of us.

"Gaul hates the light, but we aren't going to let him destroy us. Lamont built this machine from items the fireflies brought from your Paris so we could spread the light all over Rodenia. But we must feed the machine every day with the jewels."

"So the fireflies hunt for light…"

Lilly nodded again. "In the City of Lights."

"What does your mother think about the machine?" Katie asked.

"She doesn't know about it," Lilly said. "Gaul's spies patrol the forest, but they are afraid of the river so they hardly ever come here."

The surface of the water rippled in front of them, and Katie leaned forward. "What is that?"

Instead of answering, Lilly simply smiled as a pair of arms reached up through the surface and stroked toward the riverbank. Had someone come looking for her? Perhaps her dad had found his way here.

Then she saw the top of a black beret, and her heart leapt. It wasn't someone to help her. It was the thief she saw in Paris. How had he found his way into this land?

"We must hide," Katie said.

But the princess didn't move. "It's only Ostel."

Katie watched as the man shrank in size, his black beret swirling like it had been trapped in a tornado. She blinked again before she realized what happened.

Ostel had turned into a firefly.

He flew over to the princess and bowed his head. "Your highness."

"What have you found for us today?" Lilly asked.

Ostel shook his head slowly. "I fear I wasn't able to get anything."

Lilly sighed. "What happened?"

"I almost had another ring, but a man chased me back to the river."

She reached out and smoothed the edge of his wing. "I'm glad he didn't catch you."

Ostel nodded at the river. "I didn't want to leave the lights."

Lilly glanced over at Katie before looking back at Ostel. "It won't be long before our light returns."

Katie inched forward. "You stole the engagement ring yesterday from a man trying to propose."

"None of us want to steal," Ostel said, his wings pulsing up and down. "But we have no choice— "

The princess pointed toward the mill. "The others need your help."

As Ostel returned to the mill, the two girls watched the ripples turn smooth again. If this was a dream, would she wake up if she jumped into the river?

"Will you stay and help us?" Lilly asked.

"I won't steal someone's jewelry."

"You don't have to." Lilly reached into the neck of her gown and pulled out a necklace. "There is another way you can help."

On the end of Lilly's necklace was a pink sapphire that matched Katie's, shaped like a teardrop. For an instant, Katie thought the fireflies might have stolen her necklace, but it was still clasped around her neck.

"Where did you get your necklace?" Katie asked.

"My mother gave it to me like yours did for you," Lilly said. "When I was little."

Katie studied the face of the girl who looked so much like her. They had the same eyes, the same necklace, the same long hair. Almost as if they were sisters.

She released her necklace, sighing to herself. She'd always wanted a sister.

Lilly had to save the fireflies without stealing more jewelry. If her dad knew what was happening in this world, he would want Katie to help.

Katie tucked her necklace back into her blouse. "What can I do?"

Lilly stood and offered her hand. "Come with me."

Katie followed her to a rowboat, and they paddled back into the trees.

The Light Fairy

LILLY LEFT the rowboat at the edge of the forest, beside a mound of black rocks. Ahead was a long valley that swept up into a snow-capped mountain peak. A palace stood about halfway up the mountain with two tall spires climbing into the dark sky. If there was more light, Katie imagined it would be a majestic palace, but in the gray shadows, it looked more like a haunted house.

"We need to get there," Lilly whispered, "but we can't cross through the valley."

Katie scanned the land in front of them. "Why not?"

"Watch closely."

Dark splotches appeared in the valley, a sea of red lights combing back and forth at the base of the mountain.

"Are they fireflies?" Katie whispered.

Lilly shook her head. "They're fire ants."

Katie shuddered.

"Gaul has taken over our army and commanded them to guard the palace."

"I can't help you defeat an army."

Lilly motioned to their right. "We need to climb through there."

As they shuffled over a boulder, Katie realized they were standing inside the mouth of a cave. She took her cell phone from her pocket and used the light to scan the rocky walls.

Lilly pointed at the phone. "You won't need that."

Curious, Katie turned off the phone. A soft pink hue splashed across the walls of the cave, and it took a moment before Katie realized the light was coming from Lilly's necklace. Katie lifted her sapphire out from under her shirt, and it sprinkled a path of pink light along the passage as well.

Lilly looked pleased. "They will grow brighter as we near the palace."

As they walked, Katie thought about the fireflies they'd left behind in the mill. It had been kind of the creatures to give her a place to sleep and then take her to the princess. She wished she could help them, but no matter what Lilly said, there was nothing she could do to fight against this Gaul or his army of fire ants.

The girls began to climb up a hill inside the cave, and it felt as if they'd hiked an hour before they reached a plain wooden door set back in the rocks. Instead of reaching for the doorknob, Lilly leaned down and placed her sapphire on a teardrop-shaped button by the handle. The door clicked before it opened.

"Gaul doesn't know about this passage," Lilly said as they stepped into a large room. A cot stood along the wall, piles of books stacked around it. A dozen candlesticks were lined up on top of a long iron bench.

Katie glanced up at a row of bars around the room. "Is this a dungeon?"

"It used to be." Lilly sat on the edge of the bench. "More than a hundred years ago, a cruel king rose to power in the Land of Light. His brother, Prince Nicholas, was a good man who tried to help those who lived in the kingdom, but the king locked him down here for almost twenty years. Nicholas spent his days reading and writing by candlelight until the king passed away."

Lilly leaned back against the stone wall, lost in her story. "By the time Nicholas was released, the kingdom was overcome with darkness so he left on a quest to find light. The legend says he was gone for a whole month before he discovered Paris. The Parisians were having some sort of festival in the city and even though it was night, they had an entire building filled with lights powered by electricity. He found a tall fairy on top of a building that lit up the sky."

"That must have been the world fair," Katie said, remembering what the tour guide said at the Eiffel Tower.

"Prince Nicholas stayed in Paris until the end of the fair," Lilly continued. "When it was over, the people in Paris were taking down the buildings and either shipping off the pieces or throwing them away. Nicholas brought some of his friends up to Paris, and they carried the Light Fairy back here. Until Gaul came, the fairy shown from the top of the palace every day."

"Is the Light Fairy still there?"

Lilly nodded sadly. "But her light is almost gone. Once Gaul is finished destroying our Land of Light, he'll attack the other lands in Rodenia."

Katie sat on the dusty cot, wishing she could bring light back into this world. "How can we stop him?"

Lilly stood and began searching through the stack of books. Then she returned with a dusty blue-covered book and sat beside Katie before opening it. "Read this."

Katie leaned down so the pink on her necklace would light the page. And she read the words out loud.

When shadows from the north shroud
the beauty in our land,
When our rainbow of life darkens by demand,
Remember these words written long ago
To conquer the evil from our greatest foe.
Three stones together make one resilient light
To illuminate families and fairies alike.

Katie stared at the words before looking back at Lilly. "I don't understand."

"It's one of the prophecies that Nicholas left for us," she explained. "We've been waiting more than a year now for this light."

Katie read the words again, this time in her head, but she was still confused. "What does it mean about the three stones?"

Lilly lifted her necklace and leaned close. "Our sapphires."

Katie looked back down at their necklaces, glowing bright now. "There are only two stones."

Lilly shook her head. "My mother wears a sapphire necklace too."

Three stones to make one light.

She'd thought her entry into Rodenia was accidental, but perhaps she was here for a reason. Perhaps, somehow, her necklace had found its way home.

If the prophecy were true, she and Lilly could save this land together. "How can we get your mother's necklace?"

"I haven't figured that out yet."

Katie's stomach rumbled from hunger. "Perhaps we can start in the kitchen."

Lilly considered her words and then smiled. "That's the perfect place to begin."

Queen of the Light

LILLY AND KATIE crept up a narrow passage from the dungeon, and at the top of the passageway, Lilly opened a hatch above their heads. They climbed out onto the wooden floor of the palace kitchen.

The lines around the hatch door blended into the stone floor, but Lilly still pulled a rug over the entrance into the secret passage so Gaul wouldn't find it.

Pink light reflected off a collection of copper pots hanging over the giant fireplace. There weren't any flames on the grate or dishes cluttering the marble countertops.

Both girls tucked their necklaces underneath their clothing, and the pink hue around them dissolved back into gray. The fading glow from the Light Fairy filtered through the window, and in the valley below was a sea of pulsing red lights as hundreds of fire ants patrolled the main entrance to the palace. They would stop anyone who tried to rescue the queen.

Katie shuddered as she scanned the army of ants. The river—her doorway back into Paris—was on the other side of the valley, but it seemed miles and miles away now. Even if she could escape back through the long cave, she would need Lilly to find her way through the river.

A frightening thought settled into Katie's mind.

What if Lilly wasn't really the friend she claimed to be? What if Ostel had led Katie here for another reason? The story about Gaul and even the queen might have been made up to convince her to stay. Perhaps they would take her sapphire necklace and put her in the dungeon like Prince Nicholas.

She shivered again.

"Come away from the window," Lilly said.

Katie scanned the army of fire ants one more time before stepping away. She didn't follow the princess though. Instead she balled up her hands, digging them into her hips as she faced Lilly. "Why did you bring me to the palace?"

The princess tapped her teal slipper on the floor. "Because I wanted to see if our sapphire necklaces would break the spell cast over Rodenia."

"And if we do break it—" Katie began. "What will happen to me?"

"Ostel will open up one of the portals so you can return home."

Katie stuck her hands into her pockets. She hadn't considered that there might be more than one portal. Or that these doors could open and close.

"Unless you want to leave now," Lilly said quietly. "Then I will ask Ostel to open it right away."

As she leaned back against the cold stone of the counter, Katie glanced toward the floor rug that concealed the passage down into the dungeon. She wanted to restore the light for the fireflies. And she wanted to help Lilly's mother break free of the curse before Gaul ruined the kingdom of Rodenia.

Then she wanted to return to her dad.

For now, she would have to trust that Lilly wanted what was best for the Land of Light—and that she would help Katie find her way home when they were finished.

"I will stay until we find your mother's necklace, but what will happen to her if we can't break the spell?"

Lilly clasped her hands together, her gaze falling to her slippers. "I don't know."

Then Lilly opened the pantry door and unleashed the light from her sapphire to scan the shelves. Katie saw dozens of glass jars filled with different fruits and vegetables.

"Do you know where your mother is?" Katie asked.

Lilly pointed toward the ceiling. "In the tower."

"And what about Gaul?"

"He only comes once in the evening. We can always tell when he's about to arrive." Lilly pointed back toward the window. "The fire ants cluster together to make a big red circle in the valley."

"And he locked your mother in the tower…"

"Gaul doesn't need a lock to keep her there," Lilly said sadly, her fingers skimming over the jars. "He's locked her inside herself."

She reached for one of the jars and turned back toward Katie. "When Gaul first came from the north, I told my mother not to spend time with him, but she ignored my warning, saying he was harmless. Now she doesn't say anything. She just sits up in that tower and stares out at the valley all day as if she doesn't know her kingdom is falling apart."

Lilly sat on a stool by the counter. "Gaul would lock the tower if he knew I visited her, but he doesn't know where I am. I haven't been able to do anything to help my mom, but I still spend my nights in the dungeon so I can be close to her."

Katie sighed. "If I had a mom, I'd want to be close to her too."

Lilly set the jar on the counter. "What happened to your mother?"

Katie shrugged as Lilly twisted off the lid.

"Let's eat before we go up to the tower." Lilly took two forks from a drawer and handed one to Katie. "These are my favorite."

Katie examined the oranges inside the glass jar.

"There are only two jars left," Lilly said. "I save them for special occasions."

The princess stabbed one of the oranges, then she held out the jar. Katie slid out an orange and took a small bite. It was citrusy and sweet with the flavor of spearmint. She ate the fruit quickly and took out another piece.

"Is your mother wearing her necklace?" Katie asked.

Lilly nodded.

"Then all we have to do is convince her to put our necklaces together."

Lilly sighed. "I wish it were that easy."

A shadow crossed by the entrance to the kitchen, and Katie jumped. Had the fire ants decided to search the palace? Perhaps they had seen the light from the window.

Or had Gaul already arrived?

As the shadow slowly expanded across the wall, Katie began to step toward the doorway. Lilly stopped her. "It's only Black Diamond," she said as she leaned down. Then she clicked her tongue.

Seconds later, a black cat stepped into the kitchen. She had a white diamond-shaped mark on her forehead.

Lilly petted the cat behind the ears. "Where is your friend?"

Black Diamond looked up at the ceiling.

"Ah, she's with the queen," Lilly replied. "We're going up there now, but you must stay outside."

After the cat left, Katie followed Lilly down a hallway, their necklaces guiding them into a library with hundreds more books and several old chairs. Lilly opened a door by a fireplace, and their pink light flooded the stairwell behind it.

As the girls climbed the steps, Lilly said, "If the ants see our light, they will swarm the palace."

Katie hid her necklace under her shirt again, but the light was now so bright, she had to cup her hand over the jewel as well. Lilly inched the door open at the top, and they stepped inside the circular tower room.

The room was sparsely decorated with a plain bed, wooden chair, and stone pillar centered between a dozen windows. The Queen of the Land of Light sat in the middle of it all, humming as she rocked in her chair. Curled up in her lap was a small white cat, rocking with her. Katie tried to see the queen's face, but it was covered by a gray veil.

Lilly nodded toward the cat. "That's Starlight."

The cat lifted her head toward them, but she didn't leave the queen.

While Katie waited by the door, Lilly stepped toward the center of the room. "Mother?"

Katie's heart ached for her new friend. Instead of looking toward her daughter, the queen's gaze remained fixed on the dark window in front of her.

"Where is he?" The chilling sound of the queen's voice echoed around them.

Lilly crept closer. "I don't know, but if you're hungry—"

The queen shook her head. "All I want is tea."

"You don't need any more of his tea," Lilly said. "Please, Mother. I will brew you an even better drink."

The queen kept humming, her eyes focused on the window.

Katie stepped up next to Lilly, but the queen didn't notice her. "What's in the tea?" she whispered.

"Some sort of potion," Lilly replied as she watched her mom. "She won't eat or drink anything else."

The dark windows around them began to glow a red color. When Katie stepped toward a window, she saw the fire ants gathering together in a huge circle below, their red lights growing stronger.

"They're moving into formation," Lilly said. "Gaul will be here soon."

Katie glanced back at the queen. How were they going to convince her to share her necklace? And how were they going to hide the light of their own necklaces when they were so bright?

"Is her necklace glowing under her veil?" Katie asked.

"No, it stopped glowing after Gaul arrived."

Katie moved toward the queen. The prophecy said the three stones were needed to break the darkness in this land. Three stones to make one light.

"Perhaps the ants won't see our necklaces if we hide them under her veil," Katie said.

The two girls leaned toward the queen, their backs a wall to the windows as they transferred their two glowing gems underneath the fabric. Lilly pressed the three necklaces together.

Katie closed her eyes, waiting, but nothing happened.

When Katie reopened her eyes, the red light from the fire ants still colored the dark sky, overpowering the glow from the Light Fairy.

"Do you have my tea?" the queen asked in a monotone voice.

"Not yet, Mother," Lilly replied sadly. She

clutched the necklaces together a few seconds longer, as if they needed more time for the magic to work. Katie didn't know what to expect exactly, but she had hoped that light would return to the land.

Instead the darkness remained.

A loud thundering noise blasted through the windows and Katie backed away from the queen, bracing herself on the column. "Is it Gaul?"

"Yes." Lilly retracted her hand. "We have to hide."

Gaul's Poison

BOTH GIRLS and Starlight tucked themselves behind the tower door. Instead of closing it completely, Lilly and Katie watched the queen through the crack.

A man in a charcoal-colored gown blasted through one of the windows without breaking a single glass pane. The queen didn't seem to notice Gaul's presence, but Katie couldn't keep her eyes off him. His gown was trimmed with red, and his face was so pale that under any other circumstances, Katie would have thought him deathly ill. His wrinkled hands looked ancient, but he towered over the queen's chair.

Katie clutched her necklace between both hands to hide the glow. If Gaul saw her and Lilly, he might put them in a trance as well and confiscate their sapphires.

She couldn't see the wizard's face, but she could hear the spooky sound of his voice.

"Hello, dear queen," he said with an eerie calm. "How does this evening find you?"

"Thirsty."

What had the queen been like before she fell under this spell? It must hurt Lilly's heart, Katie thought, to see her mother like this.

"No queen should be thirsty, especially one as beautiful as you." Gaul pulled something out from under his cape. "I've brought your tea."

He stepped back closer to their door, and in the dim light, Katie saw the gleam of a silver teapot that he'd retrieved from under his cape, as if he were a magician. A red hue reflected off the silver, and the queen seemed mesmerized by the glow.

"It won't be long, dear queen, before the last fairy is gone," he said. "And then this land will be mine."

What did he mean about the last fairy?

The queen didn't respond to his declaration. Nothing else seemed to matter to her except the pot of tea.

How much longer would the Light Fairy be able to produce light? And once the fairy was gone, would the fireflies be able to continue making enough light from the stolen jewels to survive?

As Gaul poured the tea into a black cup, he told

the queen how her ants would help him take over this land first before moving into the kingdoms south of the palace. And then to the lands up north.

How many lands were part of this world she'd stumbled into?

She didn't have time to think about it for long. Starlight hissed as Gaul began to lift the queen's veil, weaving through Katie's legs, bumping her into Lilly. The door crashed open, and when Lilly tumbled onto the floor, pink light flooded the room.

Startled, Gaul swiveled around. Then his dark eyes narrowed, his pale lips pressed together when he saw the girls.

He stepped in front of the queen, shoving the cup of tea toward her. "Drink it now."

"What is that—" the queen whispered, her gloved hand shaking as she lifted it toward the light.

"It's nothing," he shouted, the sleeves of his black gown trembling.

The queen tipped her head around his shoulder. "But it's—it's beautiful."

Gaul leaned over with his cup, and Katie realized that he was going to force the queen to drink it.

"Stop!" Lilly shouted as she pushed to her feet, but Gaul ignored her.

He leaned closer to the queen. "Drink, you fool."

Katie's mind flashed back to Norah and the other girls calling her names at school. How terrible it felt to be called ridiculous or lame or a fool. Gaul may look scary, but he was nothing but a bully, threatening somebody who couldn't fight back.

Katie's temper flared. "Leave her alone!" she shouted as she rushed around Lilly.

Gaul turned, and his eyes lit with amusement when he saw her. "Another little girl?"

Katie stood tall. "I am not little."

Gaul stepped toward her with his cup of tea, waving it below her face. "Would you like to share some tea with the queen?"

Lilly grabbed her arm. "Don't touch it. Don't even smell—"

But it was too late. The aroma wafted out under her nose, and it smelled minty like the fruit in Lilly's refrigerator. Minty and something else, something that reminded her of the sweet flowers back in Oregon, of her home and beautiful horse.

"Just one sip," Gaul said, his voice soothing again. "And you'll be home."

How did he know about Oregon? He didn't know anything about her.

Lilly was yanking on her arm now, trying to pull her away, but her feet were anchored to the floor.

Gaul leaned down. "You can see your horse and your friends and your grandmother."

Her mind felt fuzzy, like she'd taken cold medicine and couldn't think clearly. She longed to go back to Oregon where she felt safe, surrounded by her people. The portal may never work again. Could the tea really take her back instead?

Gaul's voice sliced through her thoughts. "The tea will give you exactly what you want."

"Ignore him," Lilly commanded.

But maybe the tea would take her home, like the portal brought her here. Maybe she wouldn't have to return to the boarding school in France. Once she was in Oregon, surely her dad would let her stay with her grandparents. She'd never have to go back to Paris.

The black cup was touching her lips.

"Don't drink it, Katie," the princess pleaded.

Katie leaned forward slowly. She wouldn't take a sip. Only smell it one more time.

Or perhaps she would take a tiny sip, just to see if it would really transport her to Oregon.

But Katie didn't get to take a drink. Starlight sprung suddenly onto Gaul's shoulders, and the wizard screamed as he dropped the cup. The ceramic shattered, a brown liquid spraying across their feet.

Starlight yowled as her claws clung to Gaul's cape. Then she began hissing at the man. Katie blinked, and in an instant, everything was clear again. The queen. Lilly. Gaul and his cup.

Her fingers trembled. What was wrong with her? She'd almost taken a sip of the poison.

Starlight clawed at Gaul's face until the teapot crashed to the ground in silver shards. Red lights flashed across the teapot, and a clattering sound rocked the tower.

Then the veil over the queen's head began to glow.

Resilient Light

"LILLY?"

Gaul and Starlight both stopped and stared at the queen as she awakened from her trance, her voice a sweet, lyrical sound.

"Mother!" Lilly shouted as she raced to the woman in the center of the room, wrapping her arms around her.

"Why is it so dark?" the queen asked, her head turning toward Gaul. "And why are you in my palace?"

The wizard backed toward the windows, the cat still perched on one of his shoulders. Katie saw anger in his steely eyes. And fear.

Lilly waved Katie toward the queen. "She has the same necklace, Mother."

"How—" the queen started as she reached up for

her own necklace, the stone glowing pink. "How did you get here?"

"Through the river," Katie said. "The lights pulled me under the water, and when I came up for air, I was in this land."

The queen took her hand. "You were needed here."

Katie smiled.

Gaul had freed himself from Starlight's claws, but she kept batting at him. The wizard held the cat out in front of him, and Katie watched in horror as he threw the cat outside an open window. Then he pulled out a wand and waved it over his head.

"Hurry," the queen commanded.

Lilly nodded at Katie, and both girls lifted their jewels, pressing them together with the queen's.

Pink light leapt like sparks from their necklaces. Then it flowed like lava across the floor, the sparks ricocheting off the windows and walls. The light poured through the windows and spread out to the dark sky.

Katie tried to pull her jewel away from the others. "The fire ants will see it."

Lilly shook her head. "We don't have to be afraid of them anymore."

Gaul clutched his wand in front of his eyes as if he could shield his face from the light.

"Stop!" he cried, but the girls and Queen ignored him as the light grew even brighter.

His face began to contort, his lips pressed together. When his hands began to shake, he dropped his wand.

"Stop it," he demanded again, but his voice was weaker now as he dropped to his knees, searching for the wand.

Katie's hand trembled as well, but it was from relief instead of fear. Perhaps she really could help Lilly and her mother rid themselves of this magician and his dark spell.

"Just a little bit longer," the queen said.

Katie glanced over at Lilly and saw tears in her friend's eyes.

A loud bang made her jump, and it took a moment for her to realize that Gaul was gone. The pink light had sucked him right out the window.

The queen lowered her necklace, and Katie saw the broken pieces from the teapot and cup on the floor. Gaul had left his wand there as well.

Katie turned back to the queen and Lilly. She no longer feared Gaul, but she was afraid for the queen's cat. "We must find Starlight."

"When she's ready, she will find us," the queen said.

"But she'll be hurt…"

The queen shook her head. "No matter how far

she falls, Starlight always lands on her feet."

The light on their necklaces began to dim, replaced by the vibrant rays of light shining through the windows. Then the queen slowly lifted her veil.

Katie's first thought was that the queen was beautiful with her slender nose, light blue eyes, and pale blonde hair that was swept back into twist.

Her second thought was that this woman looked exactly like the picture she had of her own mother.

Katie stepped back as she studied the queen's face. For most of her life she'd longed for a mother who had loved instead of left her. Was it really her mother sitting in front of her? Perhaps Gaul's magic had put her in a trance after all.

"Are you Liana Andrews?"

The queen looked at Lilly then back at Katie before nodding her head. "No one here knows my last name."

Lilly stepped toward Katie. "How do you know my mother?"

"Because she's my—" Katie started, but she couldn't quite say it.

"You're Kathryn…" the queen said slowly.

She nodded. "Most people call me Katie."

Queen Liana reached for Katie's hand. "Are you well?"

Katie savored the warmth of her hand. "I am."

"And are you happy?" the queen asked.

Katie saw the glint of tears in her eyes. If the queen was her mother, did that mean Lilly was her sister? "I am now," she said. "But why are you in Rodenia?"

Why weren't they in Paris together as a family?

"Come," Queen Liana said as she reached for Lilly's hand. Slowly the girls helped her stand. "I will tell you my story."

"You must be hungry," Lilly said.

"I'm terribly thirsty," the queen replied. "For anything except tea."

The girls worked together to help her down the steps and then the corridor, back into the kitchen.

Lilly made a cherry drink, and Katie opened the last jar of oranges before taking her mother's hand again. Queen Liana sipped the cherry punch as both girls waited for her to tell her story.

Katie glanced out the window and saw the ants still lined up in the valley, but they no longer glowed red. "I thought the ants would storm the palace if they saw light."

"Not anymore," Lilly said. "They've been released from Gaul's spell."

Katie wondered about Lamont and Isabel and the other fireflies in the forest. Did this mean they'd no longer have to steal jewelry? She hoped the light had spread out into the trees for them too.

"How long have I been under the spell?" Queen

Liana asked.

"For a year," Lilly said.

The queen shivered.

Lilly took her hand. "It's all better now."

Katie couldn't wait another moment to find out why her mother had left their family. "Why did you come to the Land of Light?"

Instead of answering Katie's question, the queen asked another. "Did you intend to come to this land?"

Katie shook her head. "The lights pulled me into the river."

"And me as well," the queen said, folding her other hand over Katie's fingers. "I was born in Paris, and when you and Lilly were babies, we visited the city as a family. I took Lilly on a walk, and when we stopped by the river, the lights captured us both." She gazed out at the window, her voice sad. "How is your dad?"

"He misses you."

"And I miss him," she said softly. "Did you know you had a twin sister?"

Katie shook her head. She wished Dad had told her about Lilly, but it was too hard for him to talk about Liana. It must be impossible to talk about losing a daughter as well.

The queen glanced over at Lilly. "Neither of you knew about the other."

Lilly blinked. "I wish you would have told me."

"I feared you would want to go back to Paris, and there was no way home."

"If Ostel can find the portal for us—" Katie leaned forward against the table. "Why don't you both come to Paris with me?"

Queen Liana released Katie's hand and touched her necklace. "I can't leave this land now."

"Why not?" Katie asked.

"My great-grandfather created the Light Fairy for the world fair in Paris. The light will fade away now without one of his descendants to care for it, and if the light dies, so will the Land of Light."

"I will stay here, Mother," Lilly said.

Queen Liana took her hand. "Perhaps one day you can visit the Upper World, but now we must secure our kingdom."

They all stood, and the queen wrapped her arms around Katie. "I think about you every day."

Tears filled Katie's eyes. Her years of sadness, all of the anger that had built up inside her, dissolved in an instant. Her mother hadn't wanted to leave. She'd had no choice. "I think about you too."

"Will you come and visit me again soon?" her mother asked.

When Katie nodded, her mom smiled.

"I must speak to my army," Queen Liana said. "You two find the fairies."

Fairy Dance

THE CEILING of the enormous hall was plated with gold. Katie strained her neck to look up at the glittering light as she and Lilly moved through the maze of corridors to find the entrance.

The Light Fairy not only illuminated the palace and the land beyond, it had revealed her lost mother and a sister she'd never known. She had so many questions to ask her mother. Perhaps she could return to the palace later.

The girls reached the front door, and Katie ran her fingers over the grain of the old wood before turning to the girl beside her. She wasn't ready yet to step outside.

"Is something wrong?" Lilly asked, her blue eyes twinkling.

Katie smiled at her. "I've always wanted a sister."

"Me too." Lilly reached for her hand, and Katie squeezed it.

"I'm sorry I didn't trust you," Katie said.

"I understand—I wasn't sure if I could trust you either."

Katie studied her sister's face. "And now?"

Lilly smiled as she released her hand. "I'd like to introduce you to our kingdom the way it's supposed to be."

"Are there really fairies?"

Lilly nodded as she yanked on the giant handle. When the door opened, warm air flooded inside.

The two girls stepped onto the porch and surveyed the red ants that lined the long front lawn. In the light, they no longer looked scary.

At the base of the wide porch were two of the most beautiful horses that she'd ever seen, both of them eating grass. One had a coat so shiny it looked as if it was made of obsidian, the black glass formed from lava in Oregon. The other had a snow-white coat with flowers braided into her mane.

"Do you know how to ride?" Lilly asked as she pointed at the horses.

Katie nodded. "I love to ride!"

Lilly clapped her hands. "Come here, Starlight."

Surprised, Katie watched the horse step toward them. "She has the same name as the cat."

Lilly laughed again. "She is the cat."

"What?"

"Gaul threw her out of the tower just in time. If he hadn't, we would have had an awful time trying to get her down the stairs."

The other horse lifted his head, and Katie saw a faint diamond shape on his forehead. "Black Diamond," she whispered.

"Of course," Lilly said as she motioned for Katie to mount Starlight. "Let's visit Isabel and the others."

But Katie didn't move, quietly eyeing Starlight's bare back. She hadn't ridden a horse since she injured her ankle, and she'd never gone without a saddle.

As Lilly climbed up onto the porch steps, Black Diamond moved beside her. Then she grasped his mane and slipped onto his back.

Katie took a deep breath and decided that she wasn't going to let fear stop her. Starlight nudged her toward the steps, and she slowly climbed onto the porch like Lilly. Then, taking a deep breath, she edged herself onto Starlight's back.

Glancing back at the palace, she saw the Light Fairy ablaze on the palace tower, an ivory torch gleaming in her hand.

The horses edged around the rows of oversized ants, and on the other side of the valley, they plodded into the forest. Pale pink light filtered through the branches, the leaves glittering like wind chimes on the branches and a carpet of wildflowers spread across the forest floor.

Even as Katie marveled at the beauty, she wondered how they were supposed to see their firefly friends in the light? But Lilly didn't seem the least bit concerned. She simply laughed as she rode Black Diamond underneath the leaves.

Katie scanned the forest for both the fireflies and the fairies until she saw a pale green light blink near one of the trees.

"Whoa," she said softly to Starlight.

As the horse slowed, the green blinked again.

"Isabel?" Katie searched the forest for her friend, but instead of a black insect hiding in the trees, a beautiful fairy emerged. She wore a glittery green dress with white satin ribbons on her waist and sleeves. Her hair was a straw yellow color, falling in ringlets under a tiara made of leaves. On her wings were tiny, twinkling lights.

"Hello, Katie," the fairy said.

Katie squealed as she slid off her horse. "Isabel?"

The glittery fairy giggled, the green lights on her wings blinking like stars.

"You're a fairy…"

Isabel held her hands to her heart. "I've always been a fairy."

Then Katie saw orange lights appear behind Isabel.

"Good evening, Katie," the fairy said, bowing low.

Katie stared at the long striped robe that hung around his wings and long brown hair that draped over his shoulders. His slippers were a burnt orange color.

"Don't you recognize me?" the fairy asked.

She started to shake her head, but stopped when his wings blinked orange again. "You're Lamont."

"Indeed," he said before jumping up to a branch above them. He spun around twice, his robe fluttering behind him like a sail, orange tassels on the bottom twirling around his feet. "And this is my sister, Aleah."

A fairy with pale blue wings and long hair with a strand of blue braided through the black stepped forward. She bowed and then smiled at Katie. "Thank you."

"You're all fairies!" Katie exclaimed.

Lilly clasped her hands together, seeming to relish her surprise. "You helped rescue them."

Katie laughed again. This was a land of fairies, powered by light. No wonder why they needed the grand Light Fairy.

"Are you really a princess?" Isabel asked, stepping closer to her.

Katie glanced at Lilly. The queen, she'd discovered, was her mother, but it never occurred to her that anyone would consider her a princess as well.

Lamont dropped back down to the forest floor. "Of course she's a princess," he said.

Lilly smiled again. "Princess Kathryn."

The words warmed every inch of her.

Isabel placed a tiara made of flowers on Katie's head, and for a moment, she wondered if she really should return to Paris. Was it possible to send a message to her dad? Perhaps Ostel could take it back up through the river. Then she could stay and live a few months with her mother and sister and their fairy friends. Until it was time for her and her dad to return to Oregon.

Music flowed through the forest—the enchanting sounds of flutes and trumpets and even a harp. Isabel took the girls' hands, and they rose off the carpet of flowers, spinning together under the silver leaves.

Katie closed her eyes, but instead of darkness, a hundred lights seemed to pour out, flashing the brilliant colors of a rainbow. They spun faster and faster in the air, laughing together in the warmth of their glow.

She never wanted this day to end.

Pink Light

"KATHRYN!"

The lights flashed again in her mind, but they were retreating now, as if her fairy friends were flying away. She waved her arms above her head, trying to catch them.

"Isabel?" she whispered as someone prodded her side.

Her eyes were still closed, and her entire body was rocking back and forth. Perhaps as they'd danced, she and Isabel and Lilly had fallen from the sky. Perhaps she'd hit her head.

But the warmth of the lights was gone along with the rustling of the fairy wings. The cool air smelled like fish and gasoline, and in the distance, she heard the honking of horns.

"Wake up, Kathryn," Miss Marguerite said, and

her eyes fluttered open. All the color seemed to have drained away, leaving behind dull globes of yellow and white.

Katie groaned. The portal must have opened while she was dancing in the trees, delivering her right back to Paris. She hadn't been able to even say goodbye to her sister or mother or friends.

Miss Marguerite leaned closer to her. "Thank heavens," she said.

As she slowly sat up, Katie saw damp planks of wood circling around her. She'd fallen asleep in a wooden rowboat, tied to one of the docks on the Seine.

"Goodness—you are soaked," Miss Marguerite said as she helped Katie climb out of the boat, onto the dock. "How did you get wet?"

"I'm—I'm not certain." She shivered in her wet clothes. "How long have I been gone?"

"Five or ten minutes, I suppose. Long enough."

Her cast was wrapped around her foot again, the pain in her ankle returning. Instead of swimming into some magical land, perhaps she'd just tripped and fallen into this silly boat. Bumped her head. Perhaps it really had been a dream.

She had no sister nor was she the princess of a fairyland. And her mother wasn't a queen.

The realization made her entire body ache.

Her cell phone vibrated, and when she pulled it

out of her pocket, there was a short text from her dad.

I'm almost home.

She lifted her phone, showing her teacher the text. "Can my dad pick me up here?"

Miss Marguerite nodded, then called Mr. Andrews. "He's on his way."

She'd wanted her fairy friends to be real. Wanted the beautiful light to give life to all of them.

"Come along," Miss Marguerite said. "We'll wait for your father by the bus."

Katie walked behind her teacher, toward the steps. When they reached the sidewalk above, she started to slide her cell phone back into her pocket when she realized something else was inside it.

A diamond ring.

She stopped and looked at the jewelry in her hand.

Was it Chloe's engagement ring? If so, how did it get in her pocket?

Miss Marguerite had stopped and was staring at her. "What's wrong with your necklace?"

Katie glanced down at her collar. Her sapphire still glowed a faint pink.

Smiling, she tucked it back into her shirt. "It's reflecting the light."

Miss Marguerite shook her head as she marched ahead of Katie, back toward their bus.

Out of the corner of her eye, Katie saw Chloe and her boyfriend sitting on a bench. Instead of following Miss Marguerite, Katie turned toward them like she'd done when the man first proposed.

Chloe's eyes looked almost as red as her dress. How long had she been crying?

When she reached their bench, Katie opened her palm. The man glanced down at the ring and then looked back up, his eyes wide. "Where—where did you get this?" he stuttered.

Katie pressed the diamond ring into his hand. "I found it."

Chloe shook both of her hands, thanking her, and when Katie stepped back, the man slipped onto his knee again. Katie waited until Chloe agreed to marry him.

Miss Marguerite and Norah were waiting for Katie by the bus. Norah rolled her eyes when she saw Katie's wet clothes, but Katie didn't care this time what Norah thought. The lights under the river were even more magical than she'd imagined.

Miss Marguerite didn't have time to scold her for wandering off again. A taxi pulled up to the curb, and Katie's dad hopped out of it. He hurried toward her and gave her a bear hug. Then he held her out in front of him, studying her face before glancing down at her clothes. "Why are you wet?"

"I took a swim in the Seine."

His mouth dropped open before he spoke again. "On purpose?"

"Not exactly."

He hugged her one more time before draping his coat over her shoulders. "You could have drowned in that river."

She glanced down at her necklace. The glow had faded, but she wanted to tell her dad everything that happened. How could she ever convince him that she'd found her mother and sister in another world?

He directed them to the taxi, and after they slid into the seat, she leaned her head on his shoulder. His coat smelled like coffee beans, and the stubble on his cheek prickled her forehead.

"You have to be careful," he said as the taxi moved away from the curb. "I don't know what I'd do if I lost you too."

Katie eyed the water again, wishing that he would talk about Liana. "Did you and Mom spend time along the river?"

His arm bristled as his gaze wandered out the window to a row of shops nearby. At first, Katie didn't think he was going to answer her question, but then he leaned forward and told the driver to stop the car.

In front of them was a small café crowded with people sitting at round tables both inside and on the sidewalk, laughing together as they sipped from espresso cups. Her dad opened the door of the taxi, and they climbed out. When they got inside the cafe, he ordered her a hot chocolate, and the creamy drink began to warm her body.

"I haven't been here since…" he started, shaking his head as they stepped back out on the sidewalk.

And then she understood why he spent most of his time away from Paris, traveling with work. His company had asked him to come, but he didn't want to be in France.

"The memories are a little overwhelming," he said.

"I wish I could remember her."

"I asked your mother to marry me right there." He pointed toward one of the sidewalk tables. "She'd wanted to show me the city where she was born and introduce me to her aunt. I hadn't even finished asking about marriage before she agreed to my proposal."

Katie slipped her hand into his. "I know you miss her."

"I miss her and…" He stopped. "I suppose it's time to tell you about someone else I miss."

She shivered under his coat, and he directed her back to the taxi before he said anything about Lilly. "I'll tell you after you've had a hot shower," he said. "What made you think about your mother?"

"The river." She took a deep breath. "It took me to a magical place."

He sighed. "I suppose we all need a bit of magic in our lives."

"And light," she said. "We all need light."

"I suppose we do."

She looked back across the river, and on the surface of the water, she thought she saw the flash of pale green. And then a faint blue.

The color slowly spread across the surface of the water before it disappeared.

"Maybe one day I'll take you with me," she whispered, thinking he wouldn't hear.

But he squeezed her hand. "I'd like that very much."

THE MAGIC PORTAL

It's been so much fun to write the first book in The Magic Portal Series! Thank you for joining me in this magical place. I can't wait to explore all ten of Rodenia's magical lands with you.

If you or a young person in your life enjoyed *River of Lights*, I'd really appreciate your review on Goodreads, BookBub, Amazon, or any platform you'd like. Based on your reviews, readers often decide whether or not they want to invest in a new series, and I am sure hoping they will join us!

Book Two (*Butterfly Garden*) is on the way. I'm excited to share the rest of The Magic Portal Series!

magicportalseries.com

Coming Soon

THE MAGIC PORTAL

Butterfly Garden

Butterfly Garden

A cloud of colorful butterflies swirled over London's royal garden like flower petals taking flight. Katie laughed when a butterfly with bright green wings circled her head. The edges of its wings were rimmed with a silver that reminded her of her fairy friends in the Land of Light.

Katie realized now that her time in the magical fairy kingdom had been a beautiful dream. And a scary one. She'd wanted so badly to know what happened to her mother that she'd journeyed far away while she slept. In this dream, her mom hadn't abandoned her as a baby. Her mom had become Queen Liana, taken away to help others as ruler of the Light Fairies.

If only it were true…

Katie traced the sapphire necklace tucked under

her T-shirt, wishing it would glow, but the pink light remained dark. In her dream, she had a twin sister, a princess named Lilly who wore a matching necklace. The short time with her mom and sister had been the best part of her dream.

The butterfly flew toward a statue of Peter Pan, joining a dozen others that flew around the boy who'd refused to grow up.

She hadn't told anyone about her dream, not even her dad.

Especially not him.

Her dad was sitting next to her on the bench, working on his computer as he sang the song he'd made up for the two of them when his work first brought them to Europe. "We'll travel the world together. Across oceans, we will roam. We'll travel the world together…"

She joined him. "Then we'll find our way back home."

He looked up, surprised. "I didn't even realize I was singing."

"You sing that all the time," she said. "Except we are roaming across a garden now instead of the ocean."

He laughed, winking at her before continuing to type. Any mention of Liana, his wife who'd gone missing twelve years ago—made him sad, and Katie couldn't very well talk about her dream without mentioning her mom or her sister-princess in the Land of Light.

If only she could return to that land again when she slept. In those hours when she wished more than anything that she had a mom and sister here in London.

Dad's job in Paris had finished more than a month ago. She'd hoped they would return home to her friends and her Arabian horse in Oregon, but his work had taken them on an airplane across the wide channel between France and England. Here in London, they'd moved into an apartment called a flat for the summer break.

She'd yet to meet any British girls her age, but better to have no friends, she decided, than to tolerate mean girls like the ones she'd met back in France.

As her dad worked on his computer, Katie stood carefully and balanced in a bulky medical boot. Her cast was gone, but her ankle wasn't completely healed. Every time her leg ached, it reminded her of Oregon and her sweet horse who hadn't meant to throw Katie into the fence. When they returned home, she hoped Dad would let her ride her horse again.

She scanned the hedges that blocked their view of Kensington Palace. Then she looked up at gray sky above the statue. "Do you think the royal family ever visits this garden?" she asked.

Her dad glanced up from his computer. "I'm sure they have a private garden of their own."

She smiled. What would he say if she told him that, in her dream, she'd been a princess for an entire kingdom of fairies? "Maybe one day we'll be royalty."

"You're my princess, Katie," he said. "Now and forever."

No matter where they went, no matter what happened, she was grateful that he was her dad.

When his phone rang, her dad pulled it from his pocket.

"I'll be in a conference call for about an hour." He eyed her book on the bench. "Are you going to read?"

"I think I'll explore."

He kissed her cheek. "Stay close."

"I'll be in the gardens," she promised.

"Come back if it starts to rain," he said before answering his phone.

Katie glanced up at the dreary, muddy sky and wished it would rain. Perhaps if the clouds poured themselves out, they would disappear, and she could see the sun again.

As she limped away from the bench, her gaze turned from the sky to the Peter Pan statue. The butterflies were gone, but a host of bronze squirrels and mice and fairies banded together on the base of the statue as if they were vying with Peter Pan to become king or queen of these gardens.

Hundreds of flowers danced around Katie's feet in the breeze. If only they were fairies instead of flowers, they could all dance together like they'd done in her dream. In Rodenia, her ankle hadn't hurt at all.

The green and silver butterfly looped over Katie's shoulder again, and she watched it fly around a hedge and toward a shelter covered in vine. Then it soared under the draping leaves. Hobbling forward, Katie followed it into the arbor.

Gray light filtered through the leaves, making the spotted grassy path look like a leopard's fur. The butterfly was circling inside the tunnel, as if waiting for her. Then it began to fly toward an ivy-covered wall that surrounded the garden. Instead of slipping through the leaves, the butterfly seemed to disappear behind the stone wall.

Katie limped over to the wall, wishing she could see over it, but it was much too high. Was there another garden behind these stones? Perhaps it was the private garden for the royal family.

A secret garden.

As she ran her hands over the ivy, Katie felt a gap in the wall. Carefully, she parted the ivy and behind it were the slats of an iron gate, each one topped with an arrow-like point. She wanted to see what was behind the rock wall, but a second curtain of ivy blocked her view on the other side.

The knob on the gate was rusty, but she turned it anyway. Instead of being locked, the gate swung open quickly, breaking through the ivy.

Katie's mouth dropped open.

Before her was the most beautiful garden she'd ever seen. Flowers of every shape and size swirled across this ocean-of-color like a gentle wave. Stone pathways wove though the flowers, and in the middle of it all was a pond, its emerald surface reflecting the sunlight.

Sunlight?

Katie blinked as she stared up at the sky. Even the clouds had washed away in the magic of this place.

She crept through the vines of ivy and rounded a grassy path beside the wall. With the summer sun, it was warm in the garden. The breeze had stilled, and the sweetest of scents, an entire rainbow of them, settled over her.

If only she had a real friend to enjoy this secret place with her. They could wade together in the pool. Or she could wade with one foot so she didn't ruin her ankle boot.

The light green butterfly dove in front of Katie,

and then joined several other butterflies at the far end of the garden, swirling above what looked like an old well. The butterflies couldn't wade, but maybe she could pretend to fly.

Laughing, Katie began to skip toward them as if she might really take flight. Then she stopped suddenly—her ankle boot was gone!

Confused, she turned back. Had she lost it climbing through the ivy? Perhaps it was beside the gate.

A noise broke through the quiet of this space. Voices on the other side of the wall. And Katie wished she really could fly.

Was the royal family planning to visit? If so, what would they do when they saw her, an intruder in their secret garden? They'd probably send one of their many guards after her and lock her in the tower and...

It might be months—*years*—before her dad found her in the palace.

She glanced around the garden again, but there wasn't a single tree to climb, no buildings to hide in or underneath. Only a well, and she wasn't about to crawl down there.

Rushing back toward the gate, Katie searched for the iron slats hidden behind the ivy. Her hands pressing against the rock, she moved quickly along the wall. It was here just moments ago....

Like her boot, like the clouds, the gate through the garden wall had disappeared.

The voices grew louder, a whole crowd of them.

Without a place to hide, Katie collapsed on the grass, her back against the stone wall, and closed her eyes.

Acknowledgments

Years ago, I was preparing to travel to France to research a novel for my adult readers. After a fun day playing on the Oregon coast, my daughters and their friend Elizabeth said, "Why don't you write a novel for kids set in France?"

On our car ride home, we dreamed about two girls, long-lost sisters, who explored a magical world underneath Paris together. We thought about all sorts of fun ideas, and when we got home, I began writing. With the help of these girls, *River of Lights* became a book.

It's taken me a long time to finish this story. My daughters are almost grown, and they are writing stories on their own now. But we still have lots of fun dreaming together.

I would like to thank all the amazing young people who read *River of Lights* and gave me their feedback. My daughters Karlyn and Kiki. Elizabeth Quinsland. My niece Elise Nunn and nephew Christian Nunn. Journey Grace Williams. Paige Stilp. April Tackett. You all rock!

I hope you enjoyed our magical world. I'm looking forward to exploring the many lands in Rodenia with you.

Here's to our next adventure! ~Melanie

About the Author

Writing fiction is Melanie Dobson's excuse to explore abandoned houses, travel to European villages, and spend hours reading old books and journals.

Melanie enjoys stitching together historical mysteries for all ages and visiting fairylands through a magic portal in her mind. She has published almost thirty books including *The Curator's Daughter, Catching the Wind,* and *Chateau of Secrets.*

Melanie lives in Oregon with her husband who has spent much of his life animating movies, two daughters who helped dream up The Magic Portal Series, and a sweet kitty who keeps her company while she writes. She loves connecting with readers! The best places to find her online are:

melaniedobson.com
magicportalseries.com

Made in the USA
Columbia, SC
11 July 2021

41702103R00067